A
Pocketful
Of
Stories

Also by Stuart Purcell:

Heartblazer: Pyrats & Potions
Heartblazer: Wings & White Wolves

A
Pocketful
Of
Stories

By
Stuart Purcell

Pocket Watch Publishing

Contents

Jack

✦

Memories of a Parisienne
Child

✦

Wisdom with a Tail

✦

The Apothecary on the
Corner

✦

Fionn and the Centaur

✦

Delphine

✦

The Swing

Carlos and Carlita

✦

Sweet Revenge

✦

The Red Shoes

✦

The Wild Cat of Curracloe

✦

Brother Bear

✦

The Pizza Monster

✦

The Blueberry Thief

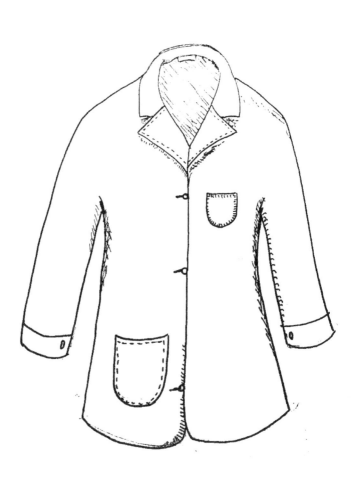

For

Ann

Foreword

These stories were written over a number of years and recently I reread them. I enjoyed them so much I decided to show them a little attention by refreshing them and compiling them together in this book.

Their inspiration comes from all different places: events I've observed, lyrics and titles of songs, anecdotes I've been told and of course other stories that I've read—I guess you could say that ideas for writing new and exciting tales can come from anywhere. The knack is remembering to keep the worthwhile idea somewhere safe in your mind until you are ready to attend to it, then you plant it like a seed by putting its first sentence on paper, water it with patience and care, let the light of imagination touch it and watch it grow to become something wonderful.

Dear Reader, these tales are ones of joy, mischief and sometimes woe. I hope you enjoy them.

Jack

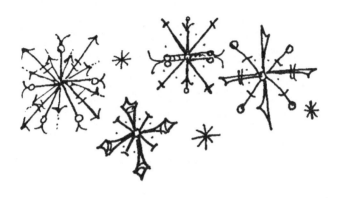

I remember it quite clearly, the first time he came to our house. I had been standing with my face pressed to the window watching a robin attempting to break through a crust of ice when he appeared up our driveway and rang the doorbell. He was a friend of my dad's—someone he used to work with. I had heard my parents talking about him from time to time. They would communicate in that funny way grown-ups do; as if they're leaving out some of the words. Where a raising of an eyebrow or the shrug of a shoulder have hidden meanings but somehow, they still know what they're talking about. I hated when they would do that as I would struggle to follow their conversation fully and instead would be left with a riddle that I had to decipher alone—most of the time I just got part of the story. As a result, I didn't know a lot about Jack however, I felt he was a person of intrigue and someone I would like finding out more about.

It was a Saturday afternoon. The world had grown dark outside for winter had arrived and she was making the most of her presence—chilling the air and frosting the trees with shards of fine ice crystals. Indoors it was warm and cosy, a log fire crackling cheerily in our fireplace. When I heard the doorbell, I bounded onto the couch and picked up my book. I was reading a Christmas annual from last year. It was about my fourth time to read it but I didn't mind, I really enjoyed it and was hopeful I would get a new one from the man in red come Christmas time.

Jack entered our sitting room. He walked slightly bent and as if his feet were gliding along our carpet—for a second I had to satisfy my curiosity and glance at his feet to make sure he wasn't wearing rollerblades. His feet were long and thin, the leather sole of one shoe untidily flopping about near the heel. He slumped down beside me on our couch sending a somewhat fresh blast of air my way. Snuggling deeper into the couch, I curled my toes and placed one foot over the other.

I mostly kept my head in my book but every now and then took a glance at our odd guest. He had opened up his coat. His waistcoat sat flat against him. He seemed so thin—almost as if he didn't have a body at all.

My father prepared him a drink; he poured an amber-coloured liquid into a small, stout glass. Dad asked Jack if he would like ice in his drink. "No," he replied, "never touch the stuff." My dad chuckled and plopped two ice cubes into his glass. They slid in and danced there making their own music as if willed on by some unknown force. For the briefest of moments I allowed my mind to wander and imagined a xylophone carved from ice, its delicate shards hammered by some powdery snow spectre. Jack lowered the drink in one, long gulp and I buried my head back in my book. My dad chuckled again; at what I wasn't sure. Grown-ups can be so weird, I said to myself.

"When are you moving on?" asked my dad, settling himself into an armchair. Jack looked bored by the question, his face pale and stern. "About a month, maybe two," he replied, "I'm not really sure. It all depends on—you know." The men exchanged a look. I tried to read their expressions but as usual gathered no meaning. I was starting to get frustrated. I needed to know what they meant.

"On what?" I asked lifting my head out of my book. It was only when I had uttered the words that I regretted speaking—Jack looked at me, a cold stare. I felt uncomfortable, why was I making conversation with him? Why was I shoving my nose in? In those few seconds I had parked the idea of him being mysterious, now I wanted nothing to do with him. I looked at my father hoping he would cover for me and maybe give me some excuse to leave the room. Why don't you go and see if your mother needs help with the dinner, I wanted him to say but instead he said nothing. He casually finished his drink, beamed at me, his eyes alive with mischief and calmly waited for Jack to respond.

My heart beat in double time, an icy numbness bit at my toes and crept up my ankles. I stared at the limp, snow-white hair of Jack that framed his blue eyes. "The weather," he said, "as unpredictable as it is, it affects all our lives—some more than others." I nodded in silence trying to convey a sense of understanding but again I was bewildered by the language of adults. Jack wiped his nose with a slender finger and continued, "I am unfortunate since the weather is the one thing that can change the course of my life quite drastically and there's nothing I can do about it. That is my burden." The man smiled at me. It was the first time his thin lips moved in an upward direction and I was surprised at how this meagre shifting of his mouth changed the whole aspect of his face.

The two men chatted together, finishing another drink. I didn't bother them again with questions. Their conversation no longer interested me; there was no more mention of the weather.

After some time Jack got up to leave. "Well, goodbye young sir," he said to me holding out his hand. I shook it dutifully—it was the coldest thing I've ever touched. I almost had to shake my hand loose from his grip for fear of my own hand freezing up and fusing with his. He winked at me, flashed me his crooked smile and sailed to the door leaving a line of crusty ice footprints behind him.

Dad wandered into the kitchen to help my mother and I resumed my position at the window all the while watching every single move of the man of mystery. He slid softly down the driveway, a billow of cloudy vapour floating about him. This fogginess all at once disappeared leaving brittle splinters of ice on everything it touched.

I now realised who Jack was. No wonder he and my father seemed like they were talking in riddles. I wished I didn't know who he was——so that there was still some mystery surrounding him. Maybe it's okay for adults to speak in riddles sometimes——there are certain things kids are better off not knowing.

Jack suddenly glanced over his shoulder towards me as if he knew I was watching him. I slid behind the curtain but continued to spy. He lowered his hand towards the ground and picked something up. I saw the crimson shape of a robin sitting on his extended finger. In the twilight, I could have sworn I saw Jack's lips move as if he were talking with the bird but I couldn't be certain. Jack thrust out his arm to the sky. The robin ruffled his feathers then took off into the fading light. Jack looked back at our house once more then vanished into the night.

Memories of a Parisienne Child

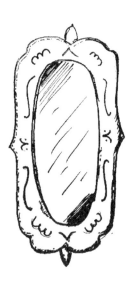

*Y*ou'll forgive me for not being more cheerful but I haven't had an easy life. We all have bad stories to share from some time in our lives when it seemed the long day was always clouded in greyness and the music of laughter rarely entered our ears but I have certainly lived with my fair share of unpleasantness and knowing I never have to return to it again, now fills me with peace.

It wasn't always like this; I remember a time when I sparkled with every new sunrise and I looked upon a world that never failed to delight me. That was when my world had Pomette in it.

I was crafted in 1867 in Paris. Around that time, mirror making was big business and I was one of many looking-glasses that lined small furniture shops across the fashionable Montmartre area of the city. I was cast from a single pane of glass, cut and polished with a bevelled edge and framed with mahogany that came from the Orient. I looked so regal back then. I used to feel so important and I loved any attention I got from snooty gentlemen, curious children and pretty mademoiselles who came to visit the shop. My single desire then, was to be purchased and hang in the hallway of a real family home.

It was during my first few days at the shop, that I met Pomette. It was raining heavily. It slung down in vast sheets, its drops pounding against the Parisiennes walkways. Shoppers raced by trying to cheat the weather. They fled along the cobbled streets not heeding their surroundings; this weather didn't encourage anyone to window shop—except for Pomette. She appeared with her father out of the rain and pushed her face against the vitrine. Scrutinising the objects through the window, she suddenly pointed at me. Could her father be the one to buy me? The door jerked open and they entered, their wet feet squelching on the think carpet. Pomette ran to me and tapped her fingers on my glass. She gazed into me and smiled. She traced the carved line of my frame playfully as her breath fell in a circular haze on my face. It was clear she had fallen in love with me.

"Look Papa," she called over her shoulder. "Let's get this one." The child had drops of rainwater stuck in her front curls, every now and then a crystal slipped down the arch of her nose. Her skin was pale save for her cheeks that glowed pink from the warmth of the shop. Her name meant 'little apple' and I always thought it fitting, since she was cute in every way. After little negotiation, her father purchased me and I was wrapped in paper, carried out the door and I was on my way.

Three happy years; that's how long I hung in the hall at the Maison Eclat. Every day with Pomette, was a good day. I don't think I ever remember seeing a scowl on her face. She was sweet and gentle; the kind of child whose every waking hour was filled with simple wonder and whose unassuming demeanour caused you to smile often. I loved spending time with Pomette and her parents and I was so grateful to be able to observe their lives unfolding in front of me: Pomette and her wobbly tooth, Monsieur Eclat playing chasing with his daughter down the hall, Pomette, her hair in braids off to her first day of school, monsieur and Madame kissing their daughter goodbye as they leave for the opera, the sleeping Pomette being gently carried up to bed by her uncle.

War separates families and in many cases can pull them apart until there is very little hope and stability left. Monsieur Eclat went to fight in the Franco-Prussian war in 1870 and never came back. Soon after, Pomette and her mother left Paris and went to live with relatives in Brittany. They were carrying their lives and their grief to somewhere else.

The day before their move the child wandered out to the hall, barefoot. Her tiny feet swept over the tiles, making a soft rhythm. She pushed the hat stand aside and dragged a chair towards me. Climbing upon it, she somehow managed to get me down from my hanging position. There I stood, tilted on the floor. Now, she could see herself properly. It was late July and the last spots of sunlight pierced through the front door and landed on the polished floor. Pomette had brought a music box and excitedly wound it up. Its music filled the hall and the girl danced for me. This is my last memory of her, for I never saw her again.

After that, everything changed. I will spare you the details of my existence but it's safe to say I was not cared for as well as I was at the Maison Eclat; I've been stolen, bartered, stripped, painted, disjointed, chipped and unthinkably, shattered. Once upon a time I was new and inviting-looking but not anymore. People seldom care for aged things and those whose hands I have passed through have ultimately regarded me with indifference and looking past all that I've witnessed, they have mistreated and disposed of me.

My time has now come to move from this world. I often wonder had Pomette remained in Paris, would I have watched her reach womanhood and beyond. Would I be there when her time came to move from this world?

My glass has been broken into a pile of shining crystals and swept away but my silver memories of Pomette are mine to keep forever.

Wisdom with a Tail

<u>Monday</u>

It was a day like any other. Alison sat in her

classroom, elbows on her desk, hands cupping a weary head. She yawned. Another week, she thought, is it nearly Friday? She loved teaching but of late it was proving a tough job.

She fired up the computer and walked to the window——the room needed light. Alison was yanking on the chain to pull open the blinds and let some morning sun fill the space when she first saw it——a mouse. It didn't move. It just stared at her. Alison halted. She dared not move a muscle, even her eyes remained fixed. She wasn't fearful, just surprised. The creature, it seemed was equally surprised as the teacher. It had wide, eager eyes, a twitching snout, and it stood alert, its paws, poised. It seemed as if both teacher and mouse had forgotten that they could move. They stood, frozen in the sunlight, two players on a stage, both forgetting their lines.

Suddenly the mouse moved. Alison expected the rodent to make a dash for it; to seek a hole or small opening within the extremities of the room but it didn't——instead it pattered to her desk, crawled up the side and sat upon a maths book. It turned its head towards her as if beckoning. Driven by plain curiosity, Alison approached her desk and sat down. The mouse was right next to her. It didn't flinch.

The animal gazed at Alison, she gazed back. Moments passed. The computer buzzed and played its start-up chimes. Alison could hear the children as they began lining up outside. The pair continued to stare in silence. Then the mouse spoke. Well not spoke, but rather communicated. In a clear but neutral voice that echoed in Alison's mind, it said, "I'm Filbur and I need your help."

Tuesday

Alison thought all night about what the mouse had asked her. It was a most peculiar request; so much so that she didn't dare tell anyone what had happened, not even her husband. She was well-equipped for the task—she was a teacher after all. Pushing all the other dozens of things she needed to remember for her working day aside, she figured she could help the mouse achieve his goal and so she made her way to work with a pep in her step, eager to assist.

As soon as she reached the school, she made straight for her classroom. Upon entering, she noted the blinds were drawn and so switched on the lights. She scanned her surroundings. Where was it? Maybe everything that happened the day before had just been the result of her overworked mind.

Filbur was on the floor this time, in front of the whiteboard. He was sliding along the floor, pushing something. Alison stooped down for a better look. The mouse was rolling a small knife in front of him, its blade catching the overhead lights at every turn. When the mouse realised her presence, he stopped at Alison's feet.

Alison picked up the knife and studied it. It was a knife like any other, perhaps a little squat in its length but no different to the millions of other table knives the world over. She placed it on her desk and sat down. Filbur climbed the leg of the desk and like the day before, took his position in front of the bewildered teacher. I guess this is really happening thought Alison, this mouse spoke to me yesterday and with that, the mouse spoke to her again.

"Before you help me with my problem," it said, "I need you to do something else first."

"Okay," said Alison dropping her voice to a whisper. She could not communicate just using her thoughts as the mouse could. She had to use her voice. And upon realising that she was actually speaking out loud to a mouse with no other humans present, she decided to speak softer in case a colleague popped their head through the door and suspected that she may be losing her mind and be in need of some medical attention. "So, what's the matter," she asked, softly.

"It's my tail, there's something stuck to it and I want you to scrape it off." Using his nose, he nudged the knife towards Alison's hand.

"With this?" said Alison.

"Yes, just be gentle. I don't want to get cut. I need this tail." Alison nodded then placed one finger on the end of the tail to steady it. She grasped the knife and scraped the tail from base to tip. With little effort, the substance curled off easily.

"It looks like chewing gum," said Alison, "nasty, sticky stuff. You'll be grand now." The mouse inspected his tail happily, swishing it across the desk from side to side. Just then, the bell to mark the beginning of school rang out and Filbur scampered away, leaving the words, 'thank you' playing in Alison's ears. Alison smiled and dropped the knife into her top drawer. She was beginning to like this new student.

Thursday

As sure as mice were mice, there was Filbur two days later, sniffing about the items on Alison's desk, his whiskers tickling each object—doing their job, gaining new information about the world around them.

Alison made for her chair and slumped into it. She immediately launched into conversation. She had pulled the door behind her so she felt more at ease speaking out loud to the mouse. If she heard the handle of the door being lowered she could cease speaking and thus not embarrass herself.

''I've been thinking about what you asked,'' she said. Filbur turned and gazed up at her.

''The question you asked me the first time we met,'' continued Alison. The mouse's little fluffy head bobbed up and down as he pawed the end of his nose, trying to satisfy an itch.

"Yes," he replied.

"Well, you asked if I could teach you…teach you how to play." The mouse said nothing. Alison ran her fingers through her hair and exhaled softly, the sound whistling as it left her lips."Playing is something us humans almost do instinctively. We all do it——mostly kids but adults can be playful in their own way too." The mouse remained silent. He listened and watched her face intently, not missing a crease of her lip, a quiver of her cheek, a twinkle of her eye. He was taking it all in, his own personal attainment of the secret knowledge of play. "There are many different types of play," said Alison, now struggling to find a way forward into succinctly defining play. She paused and pulled at her ponytail, attempting to find inspiration. Why don't I show him, she thought suddenly.

Alison held up a finger to signal a brief interlude in the proceedings and swivelled on her chair. She reached into her closet behind her and fished out an old chopping board she used during cookery and science lessons. She set it on the desk. The mouse looked on with interest. Alison then opened her top drawer and pulled out the knife that she had used to clean his tail. She lifted the chopping board with one hand and replaced it with the knife. She then sat the chopping board on top of the knife and centralised it so it leaned to one side.

"Hop on," Alison called to the mouse. With caution the creature felt its way to the edge of the wooden board and with encouraging nods from his teacher, he nimbly proceeded up the slope. The handle of the knife was cylindrical in shape and so as soon as Filbur walked past the point of balance, the weight shifted and the board toppled over to the other side. Alison prodded the mouse's rump sending him in the opposite direction, up the newly-made slope. "Go on," she said, "you'll be fine." This process continued for another half a dozen times until the mouse found its centre of gravity upon the wee see-saw and skilfully held its balance. "There you go," said Alison among bursts of laughter, "you're playing now."

"This is great," said Filbur, "thank you." Not that she was an expert on mouse expressions, but

Alison swore the rodent was grinning. Yet again the mouse had brightened her day.

Friday

The weekend was fast approaching. Alison was delighted at the prospect of a rest from her busy world of teaching. It had been a hard week. The mouse greeted her brightly as soon as she got into her classroom; their communication was seamless now. Alison had almost mastered projecting her thoughts. She now relied less on speaking out loud.

Today on her desk, there was a selection of cheeses, cream and yellow coloured wedges, just begging to be eaten. Alison looked upon them with delight.

''I love cheese,'' she said, ''but how on earth did you get these in here?''

''I'm a talking mouse, there aren't many of us but we do exist'' replied Filbur. ''Anything's possible, really.'' The rodent sniffed about the hunks of cheese.

"It's 8:15. Is it too early for some Brie?" enquired Alison.

"Never!" replied Filbur and with that Alison sliced off some of the cheese and shared it with the mouse. The pair chewed in silence. Before they knew it, the morning bell was ringing, its sound bouncing off the walls. Alison patted the mouse on the head. It shoulders were dipped a little. If Alison didn't know better the body language of rodents, she would have admitted it looked a little sad.

"Hey, will I see you again?" she asked, finishing a morsel of cheese.

"Maybe," said the mouse, "I may start in junior infants next year."

Alison smiled shaking her head. Who knows, she thought...anything's possible. Then, suddenly, Filbur said good bye and vanished.

The following Monday morning when she entered her classroom, the mouse wasn't there. He never came back to see her.

Alison was going to miss the tiny ball of fluff. She enjoyed helping the mouse; cleaning his tail and showing him how to play. She was glad she was able to teach him something worthwhile. It then dawned on her that the mouse had also taught her a thing or two. She had spent every morning with the creature never realising that the student could become the tutor; that the tutor could also learn from the student. Her tiniest friend's message appeared very clear to her now; to look to the future with passion in your heart and hope in your mind for anything's possible, that it was never too early in the morning for cheese, and above all, and this part, she felt, was directly addressed to the child inside her, don't ever, ever forget how to play.

The Apothecary on the Corner

When Bonnie lost her balance and accidentally fell through the door of the odd-looking shop that sat at the corner of Greydull and

Lacklustre Street, she never once thought that this moment of clumsiness would change her life for ever.

She had been rambling about from door to door throughout the gloomy town looking for a spot to rest for the night and never expected the door to click open when she leaned against it. How was she to know it wasn't locked? The shop looked like it hadn't been in business for years.

It was old and grotty, its windows shrouded in dirt. The painted doorframe was probably once a vibrant red but now the wood was weathered and chipped. The shop's appearance fitted in with the drab town that surrounded it.

Bonnie expected the inside to be equally shabby but it wasn't. She was dazzled and surprised all at once for she had just entered a glittering world of glass bottles and jars. Still stretched out on the floor taking in her surroundings. The bottles and jars were stacked on curved shelves, stretching all around her, from floor to ceiling, a glittering array of shades and shapes.

In the corner was a rickety ladder. It was attached

to a railing that swept all around one of the upper shelves. Standing on the ladder, staring down at her, was the apothecary himself.

"A customer!" he said cheerily, "how may I help you?" He climbed down from the ladder, his arms and legs thin and gangly like a cranefly. Bonnie picked herself up off the floor and with an uncertainty, began moving out through the door. The apothecary didn't want to miss out on the only customer he had seen cross his threshold in years and sensing his enthusiasm was unsettling the girl, he stood still and softened his voice. Bonnie who was just about to pull the handle down to escape stopped suddenly and listened to him.

"Oh, please don't leave—stay. What can I do for you? We have all sorts of things that young ladies might need." He waved his hands at the many, many jars. Bonnie paid them little attention— instead she found she was mesmerised by his hair. It was whiter than snow. Lit up by the shining jars, it looked like a silvery cloud stuck to his head. Bonnie liked the look of this cloudy hair. It made her think of cloud-watching in the summer time. Although she lived in a dull town, the summer sky with its shades of blue and its puffy clouds never failed to delight her. The sky, she thought, always looked magical. Perhaps this old man had some magic stored in some of these jars. Goodness knows, she needed a little magic in her life—especially living in this town. She decided to stay. She closed the door to the street. Satisfied, the old man smiled at her. Bonnie smiled back.

Beneath the apothecary's hair was a round, pleasant face. He wore large glasses that crept up his nose when he grinned. His cheeks were as round as his face—tinged with red, they looked like ripe, oversized cherries.

The man regarded the girl. She was a slender child—probably in need of a good meal. Her clothes were old, the colours somewhat faded. The sleeves and hem of her dress were stained and ragged. She was different to other little girls that he would see strolling past his shop. They were well dressed. He would notice them through his grubby windows. They always passed right by his shop, without ever entering. Everyone seemed to pass by his shop without entering. The girls were always accompanied by a grown-up. He noted this little child was completely alone. Perhaps, she was homeless, he wondered.

Bonnie didn't want the man to know she was homeless. Her bursting through the door had been an honest mistake. She tried to avoid trouble whenever she could. She preferred to keep a low profile wherever she was. Sometimes she felt that she was treated differently just because she was homeless. Sometimes folk thought of her as a troublemaker. And Bonnie wasn't a troublemaker. She didn't want to be treated as such so she pretended to the shopkeeper that she had planned to enter his shop all along and going against her own solid honesty, she lied to him.

"I came here today to buy some shampoo," she said, almost faltering over the words, "you do sell shampoo, don't you?" Shampoo. It was the first thing she could think of. The apothecary's ancient eyes fell on the little girl's head. Her hair was a mess. Most little girls had hair that fell, in soft strands from the top of their head down to their shoulders. Bonnie's hair was like a bird's nest. Clumps of twisted knots stuck out here and there rather like loose twigs. He reckoned the hair's colour to be blond but that it had long since lost its golden sheen. This was no surprise as Bonnie lived on the streets. Her home was the inside of an empty doorway or sometimes the inside of an empty box. She rarely had access to hot, running water. Oh, how she longed to wash her hair in hot, clean water and then maybe to sleep in a real bed.

With an agile arm, the apothecary reached up behind him and pulled from the shelf a bottle with a fancy cut-glass lid. The liquid inside was like pink-coloured honey. In front of the wall of jars was a tall counter. The top of the counter was finished with a thick slab of white marble. Bonnie spilled a handful of coins onto the cold stone. They bounced against the hard surface sounding quite like a host of drummers practising for a parade. It was the only money she had. Finding some coins in the street and saving them for food, she felt she had to use them now, as foolish as that seemed, for she had no choice, she had to pay for the shampoo.

The man sorted through the coins and threw them into an old brass cash register. Its bell rang out, the sound echoing against some of the more delicate bottles and jars. Grinning, the apothecary removed the lid from the bottle and held it upside down over Bonnie's head. Before the girl had a chance to protest, the shampoo slid out and spread across her scalp. It moved steadily, sticking to every hair. The man continued to smile. Bonnie was horrified. How was this supposed to help in cleaning her hair? This would only make matters worse.

Just when Bonnie began to look around for a sink where she could rinse the vile mess, something started to happen. The sticky feeling vanished and her hair became dry, clean and fluffy. If that wasn't strange enough, it then changed colour to a pale pink and started to grow. The apothecary led Bonnie to a mirror where she could see the whole unbelievable event unfold with her very own eyes. She watched as her pink hair twirled around and around, stretching longer and longer. The little girl sniffed the air and was delighted to be swimming in a cloud of what smelt just like ripe strawberries. She reached out and touched the hair which was now down to her knees. It was soft and felt clean and healthy. As suddenly as it had begun, the hair abruptly stopped growing and with her eyes wide, Bonnie turned to face the old man.

"How did you do that?" she cried.

"Oh, you know. A little bit of this, a little bit of that."
Bonnie didn't know— but she smiled anyhow.

"What do the rest of your jars do?" she asked in
fascination.

"I'll show you," he said, really enjoying the young
girl's joyful curiosity. "Are you hungry? You look
like you are." As if responding to the question all
by itself, Bonnies' stomach growled uncontrollably.
Bonnie nodded. She hadn't eaten since yesterday
and so was terribly hungry.

The apothecary mixed the contents of two jars
together; one was a dry powder, quite like sand,
the other was a blue ointment, light and as airy as
seafoam. Right before her eyes, the unlikely
pairing of the two materials resulted in a bowl of
steaming, chicken soup. The pleasing vapours
plumed about Bonnie's nose. She jumped up and
down, excitedly.

"Dig in," said the shopkeeper, slicing a loaf of
bread and placing two hunks of it next to the soup.
Bonnie didn't wait to be told a second time. She

slurped the soup and devoured the bread in less than a minute. It was the most delicious soup and the chewiest bread she had ever tasted. The feeling of the soup spilling down her throat warmed her up, all the way down to her toes.

The old man congratulated himself on his guessing right——a child in rags, untidy hair and as thin as a wooden spoon; there was no doubt in his mind that this girl was homeless. He thought it best however not to mention that but rather try to help her out any way he could. In his experience, when one is homeless, the individual strives to keep the fact a secret because too many members of the public look down on the homeless as lazy troublemakers. The apothecary was a kind man and did not share these views.

"Is that better?" he said, clearing the bowl and spoon away.

"Yes, thank you." Bonnie wiped the last traces of soup from her lips. She caught a glimpse of herself in a mirror. She smirked at her pink, Rapunzel-like hair, falling down her shoulders and back.

"I can't imagine what other wonders you have in this shop," she said to the man. "You truly are a magician." Bonnie walked to the door that led to the street and peeped out. One by one, everyone who trudged up and down the street passed the shop by as if it wasn't there. The child frowned. "Why don't you ever have any customers?" she asked the man, a hint of sadness in her voice.

Bonnie noted the sudden change in his face—it was the first time since she had entered his shop that he had stopped smiling. He looked at the floor, rows of lines appearing above his eyes.

"People don't like me. They think I'm crazy."

"But why, what could you have possibly done to make people think that?" The apothecary leaned against the ladder and sighed. The sigh seemed to come from a very sad place, deep inside him.

"Many years ago when I was a younger man, people used to come to my shop all the time. The front of this shop would be bustling with people buying all kinds of everything from me: soaps that smelled of roses and freshly-cut grass, medicines that treated any ailment, shampoos that cured baldness and every type of cough mixture, each one tasting simply scrumptious. People couldn't get enough of those—cherry and vanilla and toffee popcorn flavour. They would come for powders for their wigs, combs for their moustaches and ointments for their warts and boils and bunions. The place was always busy and I was always happy to mix up a remedy or a special lotion for whoever needed it."

Bonnie pulled herself up onto the counter and sat on the edge, her legs dangling over the side. She listened breathlessly to the intriguing story the old man spun.

"For years I was happy and business was booming—" He stopped and hung his head. He then pulled a tiny photo of a young woman from inside his waistcoat.

"Go on," coaxed Bonnie gently.

"Everything was going great until one day," he said, " then everything changed." Bonnie leaned over his shoulder to see the photo.

"Who's that?" she asked.

"Lottie Bell, the mayor's daughter. The most beautiful girl that ever lived. Whenever she was around I couldn't keep my eyes off her. She would often visit the shop with her mother and sometimes smile at me. I would smile back but we never spoke." The apothecary scratched his head with his hand. "You see, Lottie didn't speak to anyone. She was so very quiet. The mayor and his wife were so worried about her. She seemed happy enough, she smiled, she just never spoke. Nothing—not one word, not even the noise of laughter came from her lips."

Bonnie sat staring at the old man with eyes bright and wide as the moon. The apothecary saw the wonder there and didn't pause again lest he break the spell of enthrallment he had woven around the child. "But I didn't care," he went on, "I thought she was beautiful. One day she entered the shop, her mother by her side. It seemed she never went anywhere without her mother since she acted as her communicator. Lottie looked particularly down this day and I was annoyed since the shop was pretty busy and I could only give her a little of my attention. After convincing a group of customers to take their time looking through the range of combs and brushes I sold, I was able to leave them be and go to serve Lottie.

''We would like anything you have that would cheer her up,'' said the mayor's wife dropping her voice and nodding towards her daughter. I could see the sadness in both Lottie and her mother's eyes and at once I knew I would have mixed any potion or ointment then and there to make her happy. I loved my job——improving people's lives gave me great pleasure and I believed that I loved Lottie too.

I gathered an assortment of jars and began to measure out liquids and gels.

After mixing the medicine I handed it to Lottie. I was about to tell her when and how often to take it when the girl reefed off the stopper and much to my amazement, gulped down the contents. With trembling hands, she placed the bottle onto the counter. For a few moments there was just the sound of the other customers chattering about which combs they fancied for their hair. Lottie, her mother and I looked at each other in deathly silence. The amount of mixture she drank should have taken effect straight away. There should have been some change in the girl but nothing happened. I was just about to question my own mixing methods when she suddenly began to giggle. She giggled and giggled, her shoulders shuddering, her face slowly turning pink. I smiled at her, thoroughly pleased with the results. Little by little, her laughter became stronger until the girls searching for hair clips and such stopped talking and turned to watch. Lottie was a picture of complete joy. Her mother's face lit up. She was delighted and she paid me for the cure and quickly ushered Lottie, who was now howling uncontrollably, out of the shop. The girl wasn't exactly talking but she had cheered up and could now laugh. It was most definitely a step in the right direction.

That night, I slept peaceful and happy in my bed, knowing that I had made a positive change in the life of the girl I loved. Maybe tomorrow she would come back to the shop and thank me in person for changing her life.''

''And did she, did she?'' shouted Bonnie in a burst of excitement. The apothecary scratched his head again. Bonnie watched his hand move through his hair. She could see how his skin was old. It seemed as if it was loose, just leaning on the bones that were concealed inside.

"No, she did not," he said with sudden sorrow.

"Why ever not? Did she even come back to see you? Wasn't she grateful for what you did for her?"

"She couldn't. "

"Why not?" The old man lowered his eyes once more.

"She died." Bonnie jerked her legs, nearly sliding off the top of the counter.

"No," she squealed, "what happened?"

"She laughed herself to death. After she left my shop, she never stopped laughing. She was enjoying being jolly, so much so that her mirth continued on and on, until she just couldn't stop it. Sadly, there came a point where breathing became difficult and eventually she just fell down dead, poor thing." Bonnie, her eyes wet, shook her head in disbelief. "I killed her and now the whole village has turned against me. That's why nobody comes to my shop." The old man sat down and cried softly.

Bonnie jumped down from the counter and knelt at the man's feet.

"You didn't kill her, you helped her. You made her last few hours the happiest she had ever been. They mustn't blame you."

"But they do, no one looks at me never mind talks to me. They hate me."

"They should be happy to have you here in this dingy town. Your shop is wonderful. It brought Lottie joy and I believe it can bring others joy too."

"I'm not keeping it open anymore. Today is my last day of trading." Bonnie's little face looked up at the man and he looked down at her through his aged, sad eyes.

"No, you can't shut your shop. Keep it open. I'll help you. We can turn it into the best shop in the village." She ran to the window and pulled aside the net curtains. Dust flew into the air. She then took her hand and rubbed a circle in the grime that was stuck to the window pane. "Just look," she said, "this street is boring——everything is grey and lifeless."

"That's because since Lottie died, everyone's life became grey, they seem to live their lives through what happened."

"Yes, it was an awful thing to happen but it was a long time ago and everyone needs to move on." The man was touched by the child's positive drive so he didn't stop her.

With that Bonnie reefed the curtains from the window. The lacy fabric wafted down and landed at her feet. She kicked open the door. "Quick," she yelled, get some soap and hot water and let's clean these windows. When we've finished we can then fix up the outside. After all, that's the first thing customers are going to see and they always say 'first impressions last'." She grinned at him beneath her pink locks. The old man couldn't help but be taken by her youthful charm so he went to the sink and got some water.

They spent all the rest of that day, cleaning, repairing, sewing and painting the shop so it looked like new; now it had windows that gleamed, a shiny red door and a freshly-painted sign that read:

R. B. Thompson, Apothecary

Hair Care-Oils-Tonics-Lotions

For the first few days nobody came. The apothecary started to doubt if agreeing to stay open was a good idea at all until the evening of the third day when a customer arrived at the shop door.

"Good evening," said a grey-looking man, his face pale, his body crooked. "I need something for my back pain." The apothecary happily mixed up a sticky concoction and told the man to apply it liberally to the area for the next three days.

After the third day, the man returned. He bounded through the door, a young child on his back. The child giggled with delight. Bonnie waved at him. He waved back.

"Hello sir," said the man cheerily to the apothecary, "your ointment did the trick. My back has never felt better. The man no longer looked grey. He smiled brighter than the sun. "Do you have any moustache combs?" Bonnie presented the combs to the man and he left with not one but two combs as well as tin of camomile face powder for his wife and a box of raspberry liquorices for the little boy on his back.

The grateful man must have spoken highly about the apothecary for within two weeks of his visit customer upon customer came to the little shop with the dazzling rows of coloured bottle, the old, friendly shopkeeper and the little girl with the long, pink hair. The town woke up and got some colour back into its streets. Life centred around a visit to the apothecary's shop for that was where the colour started.

Since that first day when she fell through the door, Bonnie never left the shop; she had found somewhere to live. The apothecary showed her to a little room off the kitchen that had a neat bed and a sturdy chair. She had never been happier. She never wanted for anything ever again. She never had to be alone and she never had to live on the streets. The streets that had been, for a very long time grey and lifeless——trampled on by townsfolk who lived in constant melancholy, most of them not even remembering the reason why. But now were filled with happy faces and bathed in all sorts joyous colours, vibrant and alive.

Fionn and the Centaur

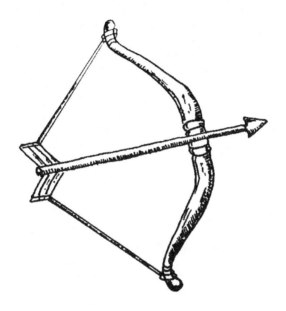

However hard he tried, Fionn couldn't keep from falling off his horse only minutes after he had got on. Sometimes, it was even seconds—he would lose his balance and slide off the saddle, hitting the ground with a thud. The people at Ray's School of Riding would just stand there, shaking their heads, perplexed. Fionn had spent weeks and weeks attending riding lessons on Saturday mornings; he just wasn't improving. His friends had started wondering whether they should stop asking him to come to the stables——it was all getting too embarrassing for them, really and children of a certain age, like adults, have reputations to keep!

Despite all that, Fionn continued to join them, all the while hoping that every new Saturday would be the Saturday when things went right——but it wasn't.

It didn't matter which horse he chose, it was always the same. The last horse he tried was called 'Honey'. The boy took three deep breaths before inserting his left foot in the stirrup, another two as he jumped up and hauled his other leg over the saddle and one more for good measure while he settled astride the animal. He would grip the reins with trembling hands and with caution, dig his heels into the horse's ribs. It was at that point that Fionn tended to hold his breath and wait for the inevitable. The animal would walk on——all good, he would think, nothing bad is going to happen. But then it happened; the horse would pull its weight left then right, in jerking motions and with unexpected agility, it would rise onto its hind legs and release a loud neigh. The frightened boy had no choice but to allow gravity to take him sliding unceremoniously down the creature's spine and deposit him onto the hard ground. Here it comes, he would think and in seconds he would be on his belly, eating dust.

It was a crisp Sunday morning. Fionn had got up as soon as he woke. He had been dreaming of being on a horse, casually trotting around a large pen. He was riding beautifully, the sun was shining and his friends were standing at the edge cheering him on; everything was just perfect. The boy's eyes sparkled, his face beamed.

Then, the dream changed for the worst. The sky turned dull and when Fionn looked down the horse was covered in something sticky and slippery. It was honey and in no time he was grabbing onto the reins trying to keep upright. But he didn't——honey drips slowly but surely and like honey, Fionn soon slid off the horse. Fionn groaned. Now his dreams were echoing the events of his life.

To detract his mind from such things, he felt a morning walk in the woods near his house would do him good and so he grabbed his woolly jumper and headed out. Fionn was so fortunate to live beside a pretty wood; it wasn't terribly big but it was big enough to wander through and feel like you were the only human being awake in the world and that you were privileged to be alone with just the sky above you and all nature around you.

At the sound of a twig snapping, (a sound not uncommon in woods but still a sound that makes one turn and investigate), Fionn scanned all around him. Autumn had painted a rich tapestry of gold, purples and browns throughout the forest. He thought he saw a squirrel vanish among some gnarly branches of an ivy-laden beech tree but couldn't be sure. Squirrels, he knew, moved quickly—now you see 'em, now you don't, so he gave up trying to pinpoint the wily creature.

Another snapping caused him yet again to turn on his heel to see the source of the noise. Spinning too quickly, he accidentally trapped his foot under some type of vine and such was the strength of it that it held his foot steady like a rope and the boy tipped over onto the forest floor. Fionn propped his head up on a wad of dry leaves and stared in front of him. He had a peculiar feeling that he may be dreaming again; he was unlikely to come face to feet with a horse in these woods but to behold a creature as strange and otherworldly as the one that frowned down at him now was just bonkers.

Steadily, the boy got up from the ground, one limb at a time, like some creaky, old deckchair. He never managed to stand completely up straight for he was backing away, looking for some tree trunk to rest against to help stop him shaking. He could hardly believe what he saw. He did his very best to hold his breath but he could feel it puffing out from between his teeth. There before him was an astonishing sight.

The creature was sleek yet muscular. It was ebony-black, the colour of coal. Its legs were longer than any horse Fionn had ever seen and they merged into a powerful barrel and strong shoulders. Halfway up the neck the horsehair grew thin and patchy and gradually turned to skin as the body of a powerful-looking man emerged. The man's face was tanned and weather-beaten, his eyebrows arching over wild, stormy-looking eyes. His nose was long and angular but swollen at the tip as if it had just been stung. Across his shoulders was slung a decorative bow and a quiver stuffed with arrows. Fionn was in awe.

"Well...who are you?" asked the centaur. It took Fionn a moment to come round and answer.

 "I'm Fionn," he gasped.

The centaur walked toward him, his hooves snapping twigs and rustling dried leaves. He then placed his hands either side of Fionn's face. The centaur looked deep in his eyes. The boy's eyes were the colour of autumn leaves, brown with hints of gold. His hair was a burnt orange, also evocative of the fall. Fionn remained in the centaur's grasp. He was aware that his whole body was still, save for his eyes, which blinked nervously and his heart that beat wildly.

After what seemed like a very long time, the centaur dropped his hands from the boy's face and moved backwards.

"You will do," he said with authority. "You are honest and honourable, I can tell now. I'm sure of it." Fionn felt he should say something, perhaps ask a question but he was still dumbstruck from meeting the fantastic creature.

"I hate to say it but I need your help," continued the centaur, "I appear to have a thorn in my withers and I can't remove it. I need you to do it for me."

"Ok," agreed Fionn, finally finding his voice, "that should be easy. If you stay perfectly still, I'll see if I can find it." Fionn astonished himself a little by how brave he had become in a very short space of time. For only minutes ago he had encountered this creature and was frightened witless and now he was willing to approach the animal and pull a thorn from its back. He ran his fingers down the centaur's spine. The hair was shiny, light glinting off each individual strand. Fionn came upon the thorn promptly. It was a stubby piece of wood about the size of a rose thorn but seemed more aggressive than any rose thorn could be since it was embedded rather deeply into the centaur's flesh and unlikely to fall out on its own. The boy grasped the thorn steadily and pulled. It didn't move, it didn't even bend. He tried again but nothing happened.

"I can't do it, I'm sorry." Fionn let his head hang slightly. The animal turned to him and suddenly looked very solemn.

"Why have you given up already? You only tried a few times. Difficult things take time. I believe you can do whatever you want to… if you just try." The animal began trotting about, stopping here and there to rub his hind against the rough bark of a tree and somehow ease the discomfort. Fionn said nothing for the briefest of moments and then, "I think I'm going to have to climb onto your back to get it out." The centaur grimaced. Fionn remembered from reading fantasy books that centaurs never allowed anyone to climb upon them, for any reason, and this guy probably felt the same way.

Somewhat reluctantly, the creature eventually agreed. Fionn stopped and looked the centaur over again. He suddenly felt weak. Was he going to be able to even get up on this beast without falling off;

the centaur was taller than any horse he had ever been on.

With deep, breaths he put a hand on the creature's side. There were no reins or stirrups to use. Fionn used a nearby tree stump to gain purchase and with serious effort, he hauled himself onto the creature's back.

From up there, he was in a much better position to extract the bothersome thorn and so he grasped it again and pulled for all he was worth. This must have hurt the centaur for it jerked suddenly and took off.

The beast galloped at top speed, through the forest. Fionn instinctively tightened his legs around the creature's belly and forgetting the thorn, wrapped his arms around its waist. Branches and swathes of ivy smacked Fionn in the face. He had to work hard to dodge them. He was so caught up in how awesome this extraordinary event was, that it took him a while to recognise that he was still actually riding the centaur, that he hadn't fallen off, that this was the longest he had ever remained on any animal—mythical or real. His grin widened and his eyes sparkled like the sun bouncing off highly-polished stirrups. Somewhere in his head he could hear his friends cheering. He was living for the moment and he felt brilliant.

After several minutes of complete exhilaration, the animal slowed again and taking full advantage of this, Fionn dug his fingers in and around the thorn and pulled it free. The centaur neighed and abruptly stopped. Fionn wasn't sure if this was a sign of pain or relief. Maybe both. He threw his right leg over the beast's back and landed on the soft forest floor.

"Thank you Fionn," said the centaur.

"How do you know my name?" asked the boy.

"I know more about you… than you do," replied the centaur, his frown lines softening for the first time. The centaur shook his head rather like a horse who is trying to offload a nagging fly. Fionn smiled but stood still, stunned for the second or maybe third time since meeting the wonderful creature. The centaur smiled back and bowed.

"Goodbye Fionn," it said and began trotting off.

"Wait, I don't know where I am. How will I get home?" The boy's smile had disappeared and his eyes were filled with worry. All around was thick forest with no sign of the trail that led near his house.

"Just follow the sun."

"But it's cloudy today," replied the boy, tilting his head back to view the sky, "there is no sun." At this point, as if by magic, the gloomy clouds parted and the sun broke out from behind them filling the forest floor in ribbons of amber and gold.

Fionn found his way home. He never told anyone about his meeting with the centaur; no one would believe him.

Next Saturday, Fionn's friends couldn't believe their eyes when they saw him not only stay on top of his horse without falling off but ride the horse with the grace of a dancer and the power of a jockey. Afterwards, when he was questioned as to how he had improved so suddenly. Fionn just said that he helped out a friend and in turn had received the best lesson he could ever dream of—even

when things seem dark and difficult, always try
your best and someday the sun will shine for you.

Delphine

The shapeless clouds pushed in from the Atlantic, a vast canopy of threatening greyness. The waves on the ocean were white-tipped today. Taller and mightier than usual, they crashed into the jetty sending spray through the air.

"I'd really prefer if you didn't make the trip, my love. There's a storm coming."

"I need to get home now. I'm really very tired. If I leave now, I'll be home before you even make it back to the bog." Donal nodded then kissed his wife on the cheek and settled her into the simple rowing boat. She wiped a drop of sea water from her face and smiled. Their dog Daobhrí found her place beside Kathleen at the helm. She barked to Donal as Kathleen rowed the boat from the jetty. Kathleen watched as her husband's figure got smaller with each row. Kathleen had taken this trip before, hundreds of times. And although seamanship was in her blood; taught to her by her father, the sea was especially rough today making the journey more arduous than usual.

Kathleen gripped the oars and pulled them through the surf. It was a bit of an ordeal, the sea unforgiving, the waves rushing at her boat's keel. Gusts of biting wind slapped against her face. The sky turned black, her world becoming darker. Donal was right, she thought. Here comes the storm. Now, I wished I'd stayed put. Daobhrí barked at the choppy sea, her howl barely audible above the wind.

"Calm down, girl," called Kathleen to the dog, "we'll be okay." The woman placed a hand on her stomach, "all three of us," she murmured.

Kathleen strained her eyes to see the port of Inis Oír through the sea mist. She was aware that the trip was taking longer than it usually did but that was to be expected during bad weather. At times it seemed the boat was moving backwards such was the force of the sea. Her arms were greatly fatigued, her wrists aching. Daobhrí began racing to and fro, uncertain how to make better the situation. The dog's antics only served to unnerve Kathleen further. The waves grew taller and angrier. Kathleen grew wearier. Water was lashing in on top of the two lonely sailors—like an unfriendly see-saw the boat tipped this way and that.

Now fully in the thick of the storm, Kathleen could hold on no longer—she let the oars slip from her hands and lay back, exhausted. They shook violently but remained in their rowlocks. The boat tipped heavily to one side and the dog was thrown towards her, its paws struggling to grip the slick wood. The animal offered her muzzle into

Kathleen's hands, whimpering for reassurance. She licked the salty water from her knuckles; I'm scared, she seemed to say, but I will never leave your side.

Kathleen hauled her body to the edge of the boat and lowered her head over. She was ready to be sick. How was she to escape this storm? She could be swept out to the Atlantic and left there to perish. Her mouth dry, she stared at the jagged shapes of the sea that dashed by. Her eyes began to close. Just then, she spotted a softer, rounder image. The image moved slowly. It rose from the water and stuck its nose out. A dolphin was skimming across the bleakness of the sea, its sleek fin visible every now and then. It was following the path of the boat. Kathleen was uncertain whether this animal was actually real. It was rare to see such a creature in these waters. Perhaps, she was hallucinating since her mind was beside itself with the fear; fear of herself and her baby being lost to the sea for ever.

Some magical instinct caused Kathleen to lie down and put her trust in the dolphin. She curled up on the floor, the dog next to her, watching the rise and fall of the boat and the sea-spray fan that spread out into the sky. Exhausted, she fell asleep.

She awoke and sat up. Her boat was nestled safely among the other boats in the port of Inis Oír. Each boat bobbed and thudded against the one next to it, a cacophony of wood and plastic. She shut her eyes and listened. Daobhrí licked her hands and barked a joyful shout of relief. Kathleen stepped out onto the pier. She gazed at the water, a wry smile on her lips. There was no dolphin about now. Had she seen one? She decided she did——a beautiful creature who had given her hope when she needed it the most.

Kathleen never told a soul about her encounter with the dolphin. Instead she declared that she had overcome the storm with determination, skill and sheer luck.

Six weeks later Kathleen was again blessed with luck——a safe delivery of a beautiful baby. It was a girl and she named her Delphine, the Latin for dolphin.

The Swing

Have you ever wanted something so much that you would do anything to try and get it? I had had enough. I was fed up being on my own. What use is a swing if there is nobody else around to push you? There were no other children on the street where I lived and my mother was gone to the shops.

"I won't be too long. You'll be fine on your own," she said. "I'll be back later and then we'll go out for pizza." I honestly didn't care about that. I wasn't interested in pizza, I was looking for something more. I was looking for company.

I sat on the swing, my legs dangling beneath me. I tried to stop my lower lip from hanging out of my mouth, to perk myself up, to find something else to do. Sometimes this worked, but not today. Today wasn't a good day—all I wanted to do was to sit in the swing and feel by body flying back and forth, the sky hurtling above my head, the grass and the garden spread out all round me.

My fingers found a break in the rope, an uneven bit. The fibres had frayed there, probably from wear. I pulled at them aimlessly before letting them blow away in the air. Some got caught in the nearby apple tree, some in my tights. My boredom drove me to think of how I could get someone to push me.

I had a plan. It was a somewhat crazy idea but I didn't care. I jumped from the swing and marched to a nearby flowerbed. I stooped down, searching. I selected the largest, ugliest stone I could fine. The underside of it was cold, damp. I didn't like the feel of it in my hands.

Our next door neighbour lived on his own. Often I would see him cutting his grass or hunched over, tending his rose bushes. He would wear a cream-coloured hat with a black band around it that nearly always covered his face. Once last summer when it was hot, the hat was tilted and I saw his puffy face. I remember he smiled at me so I figured he was friendly enough.

I stepped through the bushes that separated our houses. I chose the window carefully, trying to guess which room he was in. Biting my lower lip, I threw. No turning back now, I muttered to myself. The window smashed in pieces, the damage done. I didn't turn to run. I waited patiently at the door.

The door burst open. He appeared, frowning, his cheeks a deep red.

"I'm really sorry. It was an accident," I lied. In my head, I smiled secretly——at least now I had someone to talk to…and maybe even someone to push my swing.

Carlos and Carlita

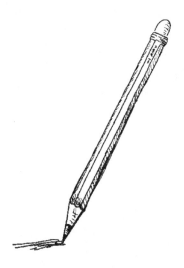

Carlos just happened. He came into being in a few strokes of a pencil. Where once there was nothing, all of a sudden, a small, smudgy boy appeared, stretching out his arms and waving them; tapping his oversized feet, bouncing on his grubby knees, making funny faces and twisting his head so that his hair shook from side to side, sending fragments of black graphite out across the page. Carlos existed now.

An empty page is a solitary space for a boy. Just think about it; imagine finding yourself completely alone in a vast expanse of white nothingness. Carlos looked around. There was nothing else in sight—no sky, no green trees or fields, no roads or buildings, no sounds of animals or smells of nature, just emptiness. Carlos had never had any of these things so he never really missed them and never wished for them. It is true to say, that while he never experienced such things, you would expect him not to seek companionship either since he never knew anyone but himself, however, deep down inside of Carlos, there was a feeling; a burgeoning feeling that grew stronger with every waking minute and little by little, this feeling began to make the lines of his drawing become darker and darker. Carlos didn't know it but in time, his arms and face would get darker, his hair and fingertips would get darker, his thoughts would get darker. Carlos was lonely and if he didn't receive some form of contact soon, it would be curtains for him; expansive, black-crystallised curtains that would sweep from side to side across his world and block out any hope of light. In short, Carlos would become so dark, his lines so bold that he would appear as a black, dusty scribble that looked ugly and was no good to anybody.

Just as rapidly as Carlos had appeared on the page, someone else fell out the end of the pencil and landed in a series of lines and curves and smudges. Her name was Carlita. She was a sweet drawing of a little girl, complete with miniature dress and long hair that was tied up in pigtails. She smiled at Carlos. He smiled back.

Carlos found himself liking Carlita more and more every day. She was amazing; she could skip and hop and dance and sometimes she made impressive cartwheels that took her to the edge of the page. She was able to wiggle her nose and bat her eyelids. Carlita often took her hair in her lovely hands and braided it up so that the thick coils of graphite shone whenever the light hit them. The pair would smile and wave at one another but that was all; Carlita was friendly to Carlos but allowed him space and sometimes ignored him. He on the other hand watched her every move and never took his eyes off her. Carlita's lines were light and fresh, never showing any signs of darkness. She was wonderfully neat and proper. Carlos thought she was beautiful.

When he first stumbled upon it, Carlos could not have imagined how dangerous the pencil would become. He jumped up at once and checked to see if Carlita had noticed his blunder. She had. But she still smiled at him. She had such lovely features——a neat chin, a moon shaped mouth and cheeks like ripe crab apples. Carlos touched his own face. He wondered if he was as pretty as her. He rubbed his cheeks. They felt flat. He looked at his scrawny arms, his wobbly knees. Carlos felt ordinary.

Carlos jumped onto the pencil and walked along its edge, his hands out straight, for fear of falling again. He began at the end with the attached eraser and walked toward the writing end. All at once, the pencil bowed its head under his weight and in doing so caused the nib to come in contact with the page. Carlos jumped off to investigate. Next to the pencil were markings on the page. Carlos lifted the pencil. Much to his delight, he found he was able to wield it and drew lots of wavy lines. Carlita drifted over to him to see what he was doing. Her interest only encouraged him to do more sketching. He drew circles and zig zags, loop-the-loops and dots. Carlita skipped and danced along the lines he had created, giggling gleefully.

Carlos stopped to look at the pretty girl by his side once more. She was beautiful. Why couldn't he be as handsome looking as her. He suddenly had an idea—to use the pencil to change his features. He had been practising drawing now for a while so he figured he could manage to give himself a couple of dimples, a winning smile and some stronger limbs. He used the pencil as best he could but it was far more difficult drawing himself with small detail than it was making freely-drawn lines.

He just about managed something and beamed over at Carlita for approval. Her smile disappeared. She shook her head. She didn't like it. He raised the pencil and tried again. This time, she looked sad; her perfect mouth was upside down, her eyes cold and empty. She was not happy with the changes upon Carlos's face. She preferred him the way he had been.

Carlos couldn't stand seeing her upset so he immediately began looking for a solution. He remembered the little eraser on the pencil. He had seen it being used when Carlita first appeared. He grabbed it and swept it across his face. Carlos was rather forceful with his stroke such was his panic and before he could stop himself, he had rubbed away his face and half his body. A pair of spindly legs sat in a smudgy pair of shoes. Nothing more remained.

Carlita hung her head at the spectacle she had witnessed. Carlos was changed. She slowly picked up the pencil and rubbed out the shoes. Now her friend was gone. Her little face was a picture of gloom; she so wished Carlos could return. She sighed and reached for the pencil. With all her might, she lifted it and began to draw.

Sweet Revenge

They had said it would rain that night and the last thing she wanted was to have a huge, gaping hole in her roof. What's more, tomorrow was judging day and everything needed to be perfect—right down to the last chocolate tile.

Berthe climbed the ladder, one hand on the railing, the other clutching a metal bowl. When she reached the hole she placed the bowl down and examined its contents; four large chocolate tiles, smooth and glossy and a piping bag stuffed with vanilla buttercream.

Balancing on the top rung, she leaned against the roof and neatly placed two tiles across the hole. She made sure that they overlapped. It will be down to the very finest detail to win this competition she thought and I do so want to win. When Berthe was satisfied that the tiles were sitting correctly, she piped lines of buttercream across them then sandwiched it by placing the remaining two tiles on top. Some of the buttercream oozed and she swept her thumb along the edge to remove the excess. She stuck her thumb into her mouth.

"Delicious," she announced. Berthe was a master patissier and her baked goods were some of the finest things ever created to eat. She had gained a lot of popularity in the surrounding kingdom. So much so, that had the proud baker kept her recipes and her techniques a secret, fearful others might try and copy them.

It was no wonder her house in particular, was

thought to be the most wonderful edible house in the whole of the forest. It stood in a small clearing on the path that led to the king's castle but was enclosed enough by trees to camouflage it. It had to be seen—and smelt, to be believed. Travellers became weak at the knees from just a whiff of the extraordinary house, well before they approached it. Its heady aroma wafted through the trees—sticky apricot jam and lavender honey, burnt, roasted nut nougatine, warming cinnamon, ginger and the creamy scent of vanilla, bitter chocolate perfumed with candied orange peel, rose petals and the smoothest, milkiest scent of coffee. If you followed your nose you would find Berthe's extraordinary house.

Why did she spend her days baking, building and maintaining a house mad of treats? Because, it was what she had always done—as had her mother and grandmother before her. She took great care to maintain and protect her house and thus her family traditions. As you can imagine, there wasn't a creature or living soul who wouldn't be tempted to chomp off part of her chocolate window shutters, or her caramel window panes or even her meringue knocker. Look but don't bite, was her motto. Only a very few were invited in to sample the house. Just like her recipes, she guarded and protected the house as best she could. The house meant everything to her and what better way to celebrate it than entering it into the 'Best Edible House Competition'. She was fired up for the judges' arrival the following day and ultimately, the announcement of the lucky winner who received a brand-new cooker with deluxe oven.

Berthe set up a double boiler on her cooker and spilled in some dark chocolate pieces to melt. She stirred the chocolate lovingly and checked the temperature before removing the bowl from the heat and allowing it to cool a little. Her cat Oskar, sat watching her, longing for a little chocolate. Lately, Berthe had restricted the amount of chocolate he ate as he was so overweight that he could barely walk. He waddled over to her, meowing sadly.

''No chocolate for you my friend. You're going on a diet.'' The cat tried to curl around her legs, willing her to give him some but he was the least elegant cat ever and because of his size, he just fell flat on his face. Berthe ignored him and examined the chocolate by stirring it again.

"That should do it," she muttered. The chocolate was tempered and ready to mould into any shape she wished. She was just about to retrieve her bird-shaped moulds from her cupboard when she heard a muffled sound coming from outside. Cautiously, she sidled to the window and peered out. She saw nothing unusual. Returning to the cupboard, she heard the noise again followed by laughter, followed by a snap. She instantly feared the worst—that was the unmistakable sound of chocolate being broken—someone was eating her house. She raced to the front door and flung it open.

There they stood, their mouths full of sponge and chocolate; two scruffy children.

"In the name of trickling treacle, what are you doing?" Berthe stood in the doorway wielding a rolling pin which she had grabbed at the last minute—just in case. The children grinned at her and continued to eat. She was aghast. They didn't seem bothered at all by her presence or sorry for their actions as other children might be. They were downright insolent and she wasn't having any of it.

"Stop!" she instructed, "stop ruining my house, this instant." Munch, munch, munch. '' Where do you live? I'm going to call your parents." Munch, munch, munch. ''I said stop. This is outrageous behaviour." With that, the young boy scooped up a handful of lemon mousse and fired it at Berthe. The gloopy mixture slapped her face, most of it going into her eyes. They began to stream from the acid. Her vision was clouded—she never saw them coming. The children ran at her, forcing her into the house. Berthe fell to the floor, her head hitting the cooker. Her eyes grew heavy. Darkness.

Berthe couldn't see properly, her eyes still stinging from lemon mousse. She blinked. She was in her kitchen. Concentrating through fuzzy thoughts, she pieced together the events that led to her fall. The children. Where were they? Her eyes scanned her kitchen. The place had been ransacked. She sat up and found that her body was strapped to the cooker with stretched clingfilm. She could feel the handle of the oven door biting into her back. She tried to move but could only wiggle a little. Luckily for her, the oven wasn't on today or she would have surely burned up.

A noise——the children were still in the house. Suddenly they came stomping down the stairs. The girl flew over to Berthe and seeing that she had come to, she roared in her face.

"The brownie recipe, we want it right now." Berthe struggled to focus on her face.

"What recipe?" she managed to ask.

"Don't play dumb with us, you witch. We know you have it——the best recipe for brownies in all the land. We want it!"

"That recipe is nothing special," replied Berthe, trying her best to sound casual, "you can have it——it's in my recipe box next to the sink." Berthe nodded to the box and at the same time noticed it was lying on its side, its cards emptied across the floor.

"It's not there, you liar——we looked. The boy suddenly grabbed Oskar by the tail. ''Tell us or the cat gets it." He hung the cat over a jar of syrupy apricot glaze. Oskar appeared to be struggling to get free but it was hard to tell given his enormous size. I like apricot glaze he thought, but I don't want to drown in it. Berthe could see her poor cat was in a sticky situation. Despite her panic, she did her best to calm herself. What was she to do? Thankfully, as if out of nowhere, a plan formed in her head.

"Okay, okay," she said quietly, ''I'll give you what you want. Reach under the sink and feel around the back of it. Stuck there, you'll find a small silk bag. The recipe is inside.''

The young girl found the bag easily and pulled out a single piece of laminated card, no bigger than a matchbox.

"Ha, ha, we found it," she screeched. The boy whipped it from her fingers.

''Let me see,'' he said. Both children jumped around. They stared at Berthe, their sly grins mocking her.

''Let's go!'' they shouted together.

''Wait!'' called Berthe, ''read out the recipe so I can be sure it is the correct one. I've used many brownie recipes over the years and I want to be sure. I'll know it when I hear it.'' The children remained silent. They looked at each other, digesting the suggestion. They couldn't leave without the real deal; they had to be certain it wasn't a fake recipe. The boy nodded at his sister.

''Fine,'' he said and began to read.

''Five hundred grammes of self-raising flour...''

''What,'' asked Berthe, ''I'm a little deaf, I didn't quite catch that. Maybe you could both read it together.'' The girl shrugged and they began to recite it. It was your usual recipe: eggs, cocoa, sugar, butter, vanilla...nothing unusual with that—nothing unusual until the children uttered the last of the ingredients.

"A pinch of goodness——what's this?" they said, their voices trailing off. But it was too late for them. The children quickly found that their limbs were tightening, their heads turning to a stop. They were stuck, still like a couple of dummies. Berthe had had them recite an old witch's incantation for those who were rotten to the core. Even if the children had got away with the theft, and attempted to bake the brownies, they would never be able to make them properly, since they had no goodness in them, not even a pinch.

The day of the judging had arrived. Berthe's house looked and smelled fantastic. The judges sampled as many parts as they could and she was delighted to hear later that day that she had won.

"An oustanding tasting house by all accounts, they had said, "unique flavours, and beautiful rendering in chocolate, especially the mouldings of the two, sweet children holding hands on the roof. Simply wonderful! A well-deserved winner!"

How wonderful, thought Berthe, a new cooker for me. I can't wait to get started on making my world-famous brownies.

The Red Shoes

She had got up at her usual time, ate breakfast and set about cleaning her house. She cleaned quickly and efficiently however she chose to leave a collection of cobwebs here and there about her home; draped across furniture, stuck to ceilings, nestled in corners——she liked it like that.

Her house was curiously-shaped. There was only one very, long room. It was rather cramped at one end but gradually widened, opening upwards into a long shaft with a big hole at one end that served as both a window and a door. There were no other windows in the house so it was dark most of the time and she preferred it dark. The house was cosy and safe, and Anitra adored living there; it was home.

Most children of a certain age quite enjoy the prospect of going shopping. Shopping, to children means that mum or dad may buy them something. The idea of shopping for shoes is one that excites and delights. Getting to pick out new trendy trainers or pretty shoes with buckles and bows would bring a smile to most girls' faces but not Phoebe——Phoebe didn't like shopping one little bit. In fact, she would run and hide at the very thought of heading out to a shopping centre and her mum would have to coax her to come along.

"Please dear," she would beg, "you really need new shoes. Your old ones have holes in them." Phoebe would plead to stay home and just play on her bike but this notion was met with disapproval.

Her mother would eventually lose her patience and Phoebe would have no choice but to go.

It was Saturday morning and Phoebe found herself strapped into the car and travelling with her mum to their local shopping centre to buy new shoes.

The shopping centre was extremely busy and Phoebe did her best to look enthusiastic among the shoes and trainers. She mumbled passively when asked if she liked these ones, or those ones over there, or the blue ones with the Velcro fasteners, or the lace-up patent boots or the plain slip-ons. She faked smiles just to please the salesperson and her mum. She really didn't care what she got, if she had her way she would have preferred to have got nothing at all and leave the shop empty-handed but she did her best to be involved since she didn't want to appear ungrateful and annoy her mum.

With each new pair of shoes paraded under her nose she became increasingly more uncomfortable and tired of the process until finally, (to get some peace), she pointed to a shiny red pair on the top shelf that stood out from the rest because of their intense blood-red colour.

"I'll try those ones. They look okay," she said, trying to sound interested.

The sales assistant looked somewhat awkward as she checked Phoebe's shoe size.

"Those are a really popular style," she explained, "I'm not sure we have them in your size. I'll just go to the storeroom to see." Phoebe sighed at the thought of having to look at another pile of shoes. She just wanted to get out of the shop. The red ones she picked would do just fine. She really hoped the shop had her size.

Anitra was snoozing in her armchair when she was rudely awakened by a loud drumming noise. What could it be? She was used to the scratching sounds, footsteps and the odd human voice here and there but like any sensible spider, she never roamed too far from her home. She found that there were sufficient dead flies around and about to keep her happy and so she kept herself to herself, remaining at home safe and sound. But this noise—this noise was different. It somehow, gave the feeling of danger. Anitra was just about to investigate when she suddenly fell backwards into the corner of her home getting caught in her own webs. The room tilted up and with Anitra stuck at the bottom of the sloping floor, she ducked her head inside her web as her armchair and table slid down towards her. Luckily, the furniture bounced off all the elastic-like webs. With her tiny heart beating wildly, Anitra watched as they slid back again to the centre of the room and then unbelievably up and over her head. She shut tight her eyes as her home was flipped upside down.

After some time, Anitra opened her eyes and looked down from her corner, still protected among her strands of spider elastic. She stared at her trashed furniture which was now sitting on her ceiling. She was befuddled as to what was going on. This had never happened before. She had lived peacefully in this shiny red shoe for months without the slightest bit of disturbance and now today her whole world had been literally turned upside down. She clung to her web too frightened to do anything else. She waited.

"At last," sighed Phoebe's mum when she saw the sales assistant coming towards them with the box. The box was opened and there were the new red shoes. Phoebe had to admit to herself that they were pretty. She stroked her fingertips along the leather. Her mum and the sales assistant watched eagerly. They were grinning at her, encouraging her without words to try them on, so she sat and began to pull off her old trainers.

Anitra had calmed down, her arachnid heart beating more steadily. Wondering what was happening, she steeled herself and crept to the opening of the shoe. Her tiny legs grabbed the stitching as she peered out. Something was coming towards her. She raced backwards, away from the opening.

Phoebe snatched Anitra's home up in one hand and pulled back the leather. She nosed her toes into the opening and slowly lowered her foot inside.

Then, she suddenly halted.

"No wait, "I've a blister on this toe from playing too much football. I'll try on the other shoe instead." Anitra who was now huddled in the corner with the cupboard barricading her, exhaled softly in relief. For the moment she was safe. She collapsed into her armchair and tried to come up with a plan.

The shoe fit perfectly and Phoebe and her mum paid the sales assistant and left the shop with the shoes, (and Anitra), in a cardboard box.

When they got home, Phoebe took the shoes from the box and left them on her bedroom floor. She then went downstairs for dinner. Anitra listened closely and when she was certain that another large foot wasn't going to enter her home and crush her to death, she eased her way to the opening of the shoe to explore the outside.

She found herself in a room with a mirrored wardrobe and a long bed. She was no longer in the dark storeroom of the shoe shop. Instinct told her to get out of there at once. Without wasting any more time, she scaled the wall and grabbed onto the end of the curtains. She was just making her way across the window sill when she heard footsteps pounding up the stairs. She froze on the spot.

Phoebe bounded into the room like a joyous puppy. She had been thinking about the new shoes during her dinner, picturing herself wearing them out on the street and she found that she enjoyed this idea more and more—they were just too pretty to leave on her bedroom floor, unworn. After all, the shopping experience which she didn't enjoy very much was now finished and she might as well enjoy the shoes.

She sat on the floor and pulled them on excitedly. Her foot sat snuggly in the first one no problem, but when she tried to fit into the second one she had to pull her foot out sharply—something was inside and it was pushing into her sole rather painfully. Her hand dived inside and pulled out what she thought was a group of rough stones. Upon closer examination, she saw that they were the tiniest replicas of doll's furniture she had ever seen. They were so dainty and with so much detail—they were quite remarkable, really. Who could have carved something as tiny as these? She grabbed an old magnifying glass from her desk and studied the pieces some more. They appeared to be covered in a fine silk not unlike a spider's. Phoebe was so taken with the mini furniture that it didn't cross her mind how odd the whole thing was; it wasn't every day you found such things in newly-bought shoes. She dusted off the little armchair, cabinet and table with her cardigan and placed them on the window sill right next to the crouching figure of Anitra.

When she saw the spider, Phoebe stopped and stared. It then hit her that the furniture belonged to the spider. Why not, she thought. Anything's possible, they say. Anitra, sensing there was no danger went and sat in her armchair. Phoebe giggled with delight.

Over the coming weeks, Phoebe and Anitra learned to live with one another and a rather unusual but yet pleasant friendship was spun between them. Phoebe had kept the shoebox and placed Anitra and all her furniture inside it. She made some little holes in the sides and a square door so Anitra could come and go as she pleased. The spider enjoyed the security of her new home and found that spinning a web in the corner of the window sill was the best place to catch flies. Phoebe kept the box hidden on the top of her wardrobe and Anitra was never disturbed. In return for the new home, Anitra never ventured into Phoebe's new shoes or any of her other footwear for that matter, ever again. She did consider exploring them though, as she knew very well that shoes make great homes for spiders. But she stayed well clear...just in case.

The Wild Cat of Curracloe

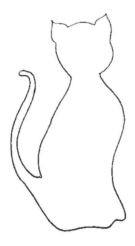

The moon hung in the sky, its edges covered with a milky haze. Although it was well after dark, the curtains were not yet drawn. The caravan was cosy; it still held some of the heat from the daytime. It had been a beautiful day——one of those rare Irish summer days when the sky is the clearest blue and the sun makes a long-overdue guest appearance and all who live beneath her enjoy life, feeling happy and worry-free.

The family had spent the day by the sea. On the floor among a sprinkling of sand, lay the beach bag, its zip undone, coloured towels and damp bathing suits spilling out. The windows of the caravan were a little fogged up, especially the one over the sink. Deirdre was standing by the sink, busily scrubbing the inside of a cup. She had suds covering her fingers, her wrists pink from the water. It was getting too hot from the steam and she used the inside of her arm to wipe her clammy forehead.

''Is that kitchen nearly done?'' called Betty, her mother, who had settled herself at the table, a cup of coffee and a box of cigarettes laid out in front of her. Opposite, sat her grandmother, Molly. Molly watched her granddaughter at work. In front of her was a tin of salmon, two slices of bread and a slab of yellow, Wexford butter. She was getting ready to prepare a late evening sandwich. She did this most evenings; it was a bedtime ritual and sometimes, if the mood took her, the sandwich would be followed by a small glass of whiskey.

''Well?'' repeated Betty, ''are you finished? Deirdre said nothing. ''I've been telling you to do that wash-up for an hour now. Look at the time, it's pitch dark outside."

"I'm nearly finished. What difference does it make when I start? I always get it done." Deirdre frowned. Betty pulled a cigarette from the box and lit it.

"What were you doing till this hour outside anyway? There's too much gallivanting going on around here after dark." Deirdre shook her head. I'm fourteen, she thought, I don't have to tell her everything I'm doing. This was true for Deirdre most of the time, however this time she had to tell her mam what she was doing outside. I need to pick the right time, that's all, she thought.

Molly opened her salmon and piled it onto a slice of bread. She caught Deirdre's eye and winked at her.

"Leave them to drain, love. I'll dry them for you when I'm finished eating this."

"You will not mam, let her finish the job. She's done nothing else today to help out," said Betty.

"I'll finish them Nanny," said Deirdre, "thanks but I'm nearly done."

 A couple minutes of silence passed where Molly ate, Deirdre dried dishes and Betty sipped her coffee; content moments when each was reflective on the day that had passed and there was no drama or conflict between the generations.

All that was short-lived; without warning, a streak of fuzziness darted from around the open door of one of the bunk rooms. It moved too quickly for the eye to discern but everyone had seen where it went. It rushed into the beach bag and was moving about inside.

The two women leapt up sending plates and cups flying. They stood on the seats, panicking. Now is the time to tell her, thought Deirdre.

"What in the blazes is that?" screeched Betty, reaching for another cigarette. "It's a rat. It's a rat!" Deirdre was grinning, her head tilted. She didn't move for some time, laughing at the sight of her mam and nanny huddled on the seats.

"Relax," she said casually. She bent down and bundled out a kitten from the bag. The animal was quite snug among the towels. She held it up to her shoulder like a baby.

"Look what you're afraid of—a cat. It's just a kitten, Mam." The kitten had poked out her claws and was toying with Deirdre's hair.

"Where in the name of God, did it come from?" Betty had sat down again into the seat and was dragging heavily on her cigarette.

"I found her, in the ditch. She's wild." Deirdre looked at the two, her eyes plaintive, her head nodding, convincingly trying to suggest that this was a good thing.

"Before you even ask," exclaimed her mam, "no, you can not keep it."

"Aww, please. She'll be no bother, you won't even know she's here." Betty shook her head wildly, smoke billowing around her face.

"And what about feeding it?" she said.

"Nanny, you'll help, won't you?"

Molly pulled her plate towards her. ''She's not getting any of me salmon,'' she chuckled, brandishing a fork at the cat.

''It's not staying,'' said Betty, ''I don't like cats.'' Deirdre lifted the kitten from her shoulder. She had to pull and wiggle to loosen it since one of its claws had caught in her t-shirt.

''Look, it'll have your clothes ruined. At least try and hold it properly so it won't pull threads out.''

''Ahh, look,'' said Molly, ''it's a lovely little thing. Look at its little, pink nose.'' Deirdre had placed the animal onto the table where it immediately began to make for the salmon. Molly tapped it on its head.

''Get it off the table Deirdre, we have to eat there. Please.'' Deirdre's mother was not warming to the furry visitor.

''Alright,'' agreed Deirdre and she swung the kitten in the direction of her mother and plopped it onto her lap. Betty put down the cigarette and cautiously stroked the kitten behind her ears. Molly and Deirdre looked at each other with mischievous eyes. The clock on the wall ticked, the kitten purred.

"You'll feed it and take it to the vet when it's sick," declared Betty, her tone indicating that this was a statement more than a question.

"Yes, yes I will. Can I keep her Mam, please?" Deirdre whipped the cat up and started dancing around with it.

"What's her name?" asked Betty standing up.

"She called Bubbles," said Deirdre. Betty reached overhead and pulled an old basket from a shelf. Its wicker was discoloured and frayed but it still held its shape. She threw it on the table.

"Well, she can sleep in that but if there's any messing, she goes back into the ditch." Deirdre put the cat down and wrapped her arms about her mother. She squeezed tightly.

"Thanks mam," she whispered.

As if fully aware of what had just taken place, the kitten climbed into the basket and curled herself into a clump of fluff, her purring, a feline murmur of thanks.

Brother Bear

When he was four years of age, my brother, Tommy wanted to be a bear. As bizarre as that sounds, it is actually true. I was eight at the time and have very strong memories of that summer when my brother went all weird on us. Yes, I know young children have vivid imaginations and fantasise about being all sorts of things: cowboys and princesses and dinosaurs and ruthless pirates with patches on their eyes, but what kid has ever decided that he would like to be a bear—no one I bet, except for my wonderfully odd brother.

We live in a cul-de-sac which is really great because with all those houses packed together, you can always find someone to play with. There's Sandy who lives opposite me—he's in my class at school, then there's Orla and Robbie who live three doors down. Beside them is a house full of girls, the Schwartz sisters. There are five sisters and they're all named after trees—Holly, Willow, Ash, Cherry and Hazel. Right on the corner lives Mr Casey and his son Garrett who stays with him every weekend. Our house is second from the end. The very last house was empty and it was on the same day when a new family moved in, that Tommy first started acting like a bear.

I remember we were sitting on our wall eating lollipops that Sandy's mum had supplied. Hazel, Orla and Garrett were swinging their legs next to us. Tommy was there too.

We were sucking and crunching away when the removal vans arrived along with a large, blue family car. The car doors burst open and out fell two grown–ups and two kids about my age. Sandy, me and the others waved. Tommy didn't bother waving and I didn't think anything of it; he's four and four year olds can be unpredictable and sometimes a little rude. They're still learning, still making sense of the world around them. I guess you could say that children are always learning but the younger the child, the more figuring out they have to do.

 So, we're taking it all in——the mother and the two kids run into the house. We can see her going around, opening all the windows. The children follow her about, racing from one room to another, excited with their new home. The father meanwhile is leaning into the car and it seems like he's picking something up. We crane our necks to get a better look. Tommy stands up on the wall, teetering on his tippy toes like a ballet dancer. With a delicate hand, the man extracts a rolled-up sleeping bag. He's manoeuvring around the side of the open car door when it happens; Tommy lets out a loud growl from somewhere deep in his belly. I never heard him make such a noise before. We all sat upright, staring in silence. Tommy eyeballs the man, throws his shoulders back and shows his teeth. The man next door says nothing, just turns away. It was most unexpected and downright peculiar. My brother's whole body seemed to mimic that of a bear and we all just stared with our mouths open, our lollipops and a sticky trail of sugary saliva hanging from our lower gums.

I knew it was a mistake not to tell at the time because if I had, mam and dad would have been at least somewhat prepared for what Tommy did next. Our street is pretty safe; everyone in the cul-de-sac is aware of the children who live there and so cars never speed and when reversing, they move very carefully. Because of this, mam and Dad let Tommy out on the road with me to play. It's safe enough but I must make sure that he stays beside me where I can see him. This is not usually a problem because Tommy just stays nearby us while we're playing our games. If it's football, he'll play by himself behind the net—using the top bar of the goal to steady himself as he walks the length of the kerb. If it's Kick the Can, he won't bother to hide but instead will crawl about on all fours and if it we're just hanging out chatting and laughing in a group on the footpath among our chalk drawings, he'll be happy to hang out too, growling softly beside me.

Most of the time he's super easy to mind and nothing bad ever happens. Except for that one day when I looked around and couldn't see him anywhere and all the blood drained from my face and my stomach churned round and round and my mouth went dry. That was a horrible feeling. Thankfully, on that day, most of the children who lived on our road were out playing and we all rallied together to find Tommy. After about two minutes, Garrett hollers up the road from his driveway to say that he had found him. I raced down the road and oh what a sight that greeted me.

Garrett's dad, Mr Casey loves his garden and in the centre of his lawn is a pretty, little pond and rockery. For safety reasons Mr Casey had a heavy steel grate fitted over the pond to stop any children from accidentally drowning there. The pond was teeming with fat, golden koi and I'm sorry to say, but my brother the bear was snarling and attempting to scoop out Mr Casey's beloved goldfish with his stubby paws and goodness knows he would probably try and kill them like a real bear if given the chance. Needless to say, this event was reported to mam and dad in detail, not only by me but by an agitated Mr Casey too.

Soon after that, Tommy refused to walk on two legs, spoke only in rasping words where he showed his teeth and scrunched up his nose and insisted in sleeping on a duvet under the stairs; he said it was his bear cave and he no longer needed his bunk bed. Mam and Dad let him——what else could they do; he needed his sleep and once he wasn't harming himself it all seemed perfectly fine however, even though I'm only eight, I could see shreds of doubt and wisps of worry in my parents' eyes. They knew and I knew that such behaviour wasn't entirely normal.

That summer was long and warm and bright for so much of the day that little by little, we got to know the children who moved in next door——Julia and Sam and it didn't take them very long to feel like part of the gang. I always presumed there were just the two of them at home with their parents until one afternoon during a game of rounders, one of them, (I can't remember which), mentioned a boy at home named Zach.

"So you've a little brother?" I said, gripping the baseball bat and steadying my stance.

"Yeah," replied Sam, disinterest in his voice. In fairness to him, he was just about to bowl at me and I was on my second strike. We had been arguing that the teams were uneven when one of them says that their parents would really love if Zach would come out to play too.

"Why, won't he come out? " I asked. Sam ignored me and threw the ball. I was lucky this time and hit it perfectly for it made a thwack sound and rose up over our heads and headed towards old Mrs Crowley's garden five doors down. Satisfied with the hit, I took off around the diamond shape that was made up of one baseball cap and three tracksuit tops. There was a scatter of legs and arms as everyone on Sam's team scrambled to retrieve the ball. It was nowhere to be seen, buried deep in Mrs Crowley's dahlias, but we didn't know that.

After ten minutes of looking for the ball we were pretty tired. Hazel ran home to get some iced lollies from her freezer. We sat down on the kerbside and ate them, the luscious, melting juice trickling down our throats was delicious and just what was needed to cool us down. No less curious than any other eight year old, I brought up the subject of our next door neighbour's kid brother.

"Your little brother, Zach, why can't he come outdoors? Is he sick?" Julia began to chuckle.

"Depends what you mean by sick," said Sam. I considered this remark for a minute, biting hard on my iced lolly. Down the street, I could see old Mrs Crawley had emerged from her neat house and was shuffling about in her garden. She was stooping down, attending to something. Probably, checking her dahlias I thought. I popped the last piece of ice pop in my mouth and licked the stick. Suddenly, I bolted upright.

"Tommy!" I gasped. "Where is he?" Like a troop of highly trained infantry, my friends quickly stirred themselves and expertly began dashing about the road, searching——it wasn't the first time I had lost sight of my little brother. I sprinted up to the top of the road. While passing Mrs Crawley's I spotted him. He was lying on his back, purring like a cat, (or more like a friendly bear) while Mrs Crawley fed him spoonfuls of honey and tickled him behind the ears. I gazed at the strange scene and let out a breath of complete relief for the second time in so many weeks. Within seconds, Sam, Julia and the others stumbled up to Mrs Crawley's garden wall and stared in amazement.

"What's he doing?" said Julia.

"He thinks he's a bear," I sighed.

"Cool," she said, smiling.

"You mean you don't find that weird?" I asked, shaking my head.

"Not really. Earlier you were asking about my brother and why he doesn't come out. Well, the truth is..." Here she began laughing again. And then Sam started to laugh too. They chuckled while I stared at them, waiting for an explanation. "He lives in a sleeping bag and won't come out of it, except to use the bathroom." My face must have been creased with utter confusion because Sam then adds, "he thinks he's a caterpillar."

Later that evening, I recalled Sam and Julia's first day they moved in and their dad lifting a bundle of something out of the car. Of course that must have been Zach, the human caterpillar. I smirked under my bed covers thinking of those two little boys; one living in a sleeping bag and the another sleeping under the stairs, not to mention trying to catch goldfish from a local pond, growling at strangers and accepting spoonfuls of honey from an old lady. This got me thinking and very quickly a plan started to take shape in my head.

"No, no," yelled dad when I put my plan to him, "he needs more than that. Your mother and I feel he needs medical assistance. Imagination in a young boy is all very well but when his behaviour could endanger him or perhaps slow up his social and intellectual development, we need to take serious measures." I guess I could see what they were saying—Tommy still kicked up a fuss if he was asked to sleep in his bed and lately he was hardly using any English. He would just gesture with his hand and grunt. It seemed the poor kid really believed that he was an actual bear. Even so, I wouldn't let it go. I was a plucky kid and I felt it was worth the risk of getting into trouble so despite my parents' wishes, I put my plan into action.

In order for it to work, I had to rely on the help of Julia and Sam. Their little brother Zach was a key part of the plan, in actual fact, I couldn't make it happen without him. After chatting with Sam and Julia about our brothers, I convinced them that since both boys thought they were creatures, having them get together would be at the very least, interesting to observe—even if nothing good came of it. I guess I wanted Tommy to meet another kid who also took his imagination too far. I thought maybe if Tommy saw that Zach was living inside a sleeping bag all day, he might snap out of his bear obsession and sleep in his bed and start talking to us again and make Mam and Dad stop worrying.

It was Tuesday and Zach was due to go see the doctor in the afternoon. Before he left in the car with my parents, I sneakily brought him by the hand into next door's garden.

At the same time, Sam and Julia took two ends of Zach's sleeping bag and dragged their brother out through the front door and deposited him onto their front lawn. There sat both boys, my brother growling at Zach, Zach's face peeping out through the opening in the sleeping bag, pretending to chomp on a tasty leaf. Neither looked any way pleased to see the other and I cast my head down feeling like I had failed when all of a sudden, something wonderful happened; Tommy spoke.

"What are you supposed to be?" he asked, his eyes squinting in confusion.

"A caterpillar, what about you?"

"A bear but I'm fed up with that now. I want to be something else. Can I be a caterpillar too. Will you teach me?" Zach's face brightened.

"Sure," he said, unzipping the sleeping, "hop in. But I'm only going to be a caterpillar for another little while because today I'll be turning into a beautiful butterfly." Tommy looked in awe.

"Will I turn into a butterfly too?" he asked, his voice peppered with excitement.

"I guess so...oh, oh, it's happening now." And with that both boys jumped out from the folds of fabric and pranced around the garden on their toes, fluttering their arms gracefully.

"We're butterflies!" they shouted in jubilation. Julia, Sam and I laughed and gave each other a knowing smile that said: wow but aren't they weird and wonderful and thank goodness they're talking to each other. Behind the curtains in our sitting room I spied Mam and Dad quietly taking in the proceedings.

After that, things changed. My parents still brought Tommy to the doctor who said that he was just fine—a perfect little boy with a perfectly wonderful imagination and all that he would ever need was just plenty of love.

Tommy and Zach became best buddies and they play all the time now—not only with each other but with the rest of us kids on the road too. Both sets of parents are really happy that their boys are doing well. My wonderful brother and his equally funny friend keep life interesting for everyone on our road; this week they're kangaroos and after that, who knows; they may move on from animals and soon we could have pirates or superheroes or train drivers or explorers roaming around us. The best part about it all is that they are exploring it all together as two friends and not on their own. Their imagination is still strong, ever-changing and they are as weird and as unpredictable as ever. I hope they never change.

The Pizza Monster

Holly and Robbie's Aunt Suzie's back garden was long and thin. It was so long that only half of it was actually maintained. It was mostly tidy and beautiful: a lush lawn, dainty fruit trees and dozens of busy shrubs and flowerbeds that were packed with many glorious flowers. However, right at the bottom past the apple trees it was filled with overgrown tall grasses and wild flowers. It was a truly untidy sight and most people who visited the house rarely bothered to wander there at all.

The children enjoyed visiting their aunt, not only because they adored her but also because of the garden. It was a wonderful, adventurous space in which they could have endless games of hide and seek and even though there were just the two of them during these games, it was never dull because of the size and interest the remarkable garden held.

It was a sunny Saturday afternoon and Suzie had promised the children that they were all going to make some pizzas—not shop-bought ones she said but proper home-made ones using real yeast.

After washing their hands, the children gathered at her square kitchen table and helped with making the dough. Flour, oil, yeast, warm water and a little salt were combined together in a large bowl. Suzie worked it together to make a rough dough then gave each child a piece. The twins stretched and squeezed the dough until it was silky and flexible then their aunt popped it back into the bowl and covered it with a clean tea towel.

''What happens now?'' cried Holly clapping her hands, chunks of dough flying into the air.

''We allow it to rise?'' Robbie looked perplexed.

''What's going to rise?'' he asked. Suzie picked up a cloth and began to wipe down the table.

''The dough needs to rise. You see, the yeast that we put into the dough is alive and it creates gas that will make the dough puff up like a balloon.'' The twins' eyes widened, their noses crinkled causing their freckles to briefly disappear in the creases.

''You mean, our dough is like a creature or a monster,'' said Robbie in a whisper. Suzie laughed.

''Yes, I suppose so.'' She stopped wiping and leaned across the table to her niece and nephew.

''Do you like monsters?'' she said softly, showing her two front teeth slowly.

"Nooo!" they cried dashing from the table and running away down the garden screaming with glee." Suzie chuckled as she continued to clean off the table. She had been doing the monster routine since they were old enough to talk. She only had to bare her front two teeth or utter the word 'monster' and the pair were off, scrambling from her clutches; a little in fear but mostly in complete enjoyment. Who didn't love being chased around and then caught and tickled? Suzie walked to the back door and waved. The children were right at the bottom waiting for her to follow.

"Hey, while you're down there, will you pick some fresh herbs for the top of our pizza?" The twins waved. They had picked herbs for their cooking before so they knew exactly which ones to choose.

"Let's get some sage and some of that lemon thyme," said Holly pulling up a handful of leaves.

"Okay. What about some oregano too. We put that on our pasta the last time we cooked with Aunt Suzie."

"Okay but I can't see it right now." Holly was crouching down, naming off the herbs she recognised. "Thyme, marjoram, sage, rosemary, parsley, chives…" She stopped. "It's not here."

"I thought we picked it the last time," said Robbie, looking beyond the herb garden. He stepped past the apple trees and into the unkempt scrub that lay beyond.

"Here's some," he shouted. Holly sprinted over to him and they both hovered over the plant. Holly picked off a bit and rubbed it between her fingers. She sniffed the torn leaf.

"It's smells lovely but I'm not sure it's oregano. Let's pick some anyway." Holly yanked out a sprig and placed it in her pocket.

"I wouldn't pick that. Pick that and you're asking for trouble." The children nearly jumped out of their skins. A rasping voice came from next door. Down near the extreme end of the garden walking through a gap in the fence towards them with a cane, was a woman. She had green wellington boots on and a large grey coat even though it was a sunny, dry day. Her face was round and fat and it sat beneath a cropped bush of curls. On her head was a straw hat laden with brown, dried flowers.

She seemed no different to any other woman but her very appearance in the garden caused the children to shuffle backwards. The woman still approached. The twins backed into the rustling leaves of the apple trees. They stopped, blocked by the branches.

"It's still in your pocket," said the woman pointing at Holly. Holly didn't reply. She grabbed her brother's hand.

"Well, didn't you hear me, that leaf you have, give it to me. It not's safe to hold onto." The woman made a sudden jerking motion towards the children, her walking cane outstretched. This was the final fearful straw for Robbie and Holly. Without speaking, they made the briefest eye contact and then were gone, racing up the garden to the house, hands still locked together tightly.

They burst through the kitchen door in a torrent of jittery chatter.

"There was an old woman...she wanted the herbs I picked...she said we were asking for trouble...she's chasing us..."

"Slow down, slow down," said Suzie, waving her hands.

"Close the door, she's coming. She's following us," screeched Holly.

"Who is?"

"The woman next door." Suzie stepped out onto the lawn and used her palm to shade her eyes from the sun. She peered down to the end of the garden.

"There's nobody there."

"Your neighbour from next door," said Robbie.

"But nobody lives next door. It's a rental house. Has been for years and no one is living in it right now."

"You're joking," said the twins at the same time, trying to see out the door over their aunt's shoulders.

"Well, there's nobody around. You must have been mistaken, too much sun or something. You're hallucinating." This was met with another torrent of emphatic reassurances that the woman was real and had spoken to the children and was super creepy.

"Okay," Suzie said, "I believe you but let's forget about it now. We have pizza to bake. Did you get the herbs?" Suzie reached into her pocket and pulled out a fistful of green leaves and stalks.

"She wanted one of these leaves that we picked," said Robbie. He picked up the herb and sniffed it. Suzie took it from him and studied it.

"Mmhh," she said, "it's not oregano but it smells really good. Let's use some of it." The twins looked at each other and shrugged.

Once the pizza dough was divided up and shaped, spread with tomato sauce, topped with peppers, salami, and mozzarella and sprinkled with the herbs, it was placed into a hot oven to bake.

The children and their aunt cleaned up, set the table and watched TV until the pizza was ready.

There was calm in the house, which was especially welcome after the dramatic episode in the garden; the comforting sound of the television babbled away, a delicious waft of pizza sailed through the air, the children relaxed, eyes glued to the screen and Suzie dozed with her feet up.

BANG! They all leapt up off the sofa. The sound had come from the kitchen. They ran to investigate. BANG! It was coming from the oven. A little cautiously, (just in case), Suzie moved toward the oven door. The oven was at eye level so she had an excellent view of the inside. She peered in. Everything looked normal; the pizza was crisping up at the edges, the cheese molten and starting to brown. The children crept behind her. Slowly Suzie grasped the handle of the door and opened it. Nothing unusual, just one delicious pizza.

Suzie looked at the children and smiled. WHOOSH! Just when she was about to shut the oven door again, the pizza whizzed by her head like a discus flung by an Olympian athlete of ancient Greece. It landed SLAP, on the table. The twins and Suzie crept to the table for a better look. The pizza immediately began to change shape, its circular form pushing out in several different places, creating a sort of pizza mess.

Instinctively, Suzie and the twins backed away from the morphing pizza. It seemed to be alive. Squelching in dripping cheese, it rose up towards the ceiling. The topping began to slide off— all but two pieces of salami hit the table followed by a several ropes of stringy cheese. A gurgling sound came from the pizza, tomato sauce spitting out from around a hole that had formed in the centre. The pieces of salami seemed to quiver and blink. Now the pizza had two eyes and a mouth.

''It's a monster,'' cried Holly, ''a pizza monster.'' With that, the monster spoke—a cheesy, bubbling, hideous voice that would make your skin crawl.

''You were going to eat me,'' it whined, ''now, I am going to eat you.'' It rose to the ceiling then jumped all at once across the kitchen, tomato sauce spattering the children and their aunt. They ran screaming towards the door to the sitting room.

''Oh no you don't,'' gurgled the pizza and like an insane octopus, it flung out an oily arm across the doorway.

The children were beside themselves with fear. Suzie held them close to her, all the time wondering, as the adult, what she could do to get them out of this dangerous situation. The cheesy fingers of the pizza began to reach out and grab for them. The children screamed.

Suddenly the back door banged open. A figure was standing there, calm as can be. It was the woman from the end of the garden. She took the scene in quickly and reaching into her hat, she pulled out a long pin. She ran screaming at the pizza aiming for its face. The pizza monster was completely taken by surprise and didn't see her coming. She planted the pin into its salami eye. The eye was stuck firmly in the pin but this didn't seem to deter the pizza; it laughed maniacally. Suzie and the kids took the old woman's lead and grabbed for sharp utensils from the closest drawer to them: a meat fork, carving knife, potato peeler, and some kebab skewers were all used to jab into the approaching arms of the pizza.

"It's not stopping," shouted Suzie above the mad laughter of the horrific fast food.

"I have an idea," shouted the old woman and still holding the pin with the salami on it, she popped the meat into her mouth.

"Delicious!" she cooed. Just then, the monster howled out in pain. "Quick everyone, start eating it." It seemed absurd to eat this hideous thing. It was something they had never encountered before and goodness knows what eating it might do to their insides, however, they were being held ransom to the cheese tentacles of a pizza and it was way past dinner time so anything to get out of this mess, was worth a shot.

"Let's eat," screamed Suzie and she dragged a flap of gooey pizza towards her mouth and began to chomp. In seconds, the children, their aunt and the old woman were devouring the pizza and in no time it was gone, its screams and its evil ways eaten and trapped in their stomachs.

"Thank goodness for that," sighed Suzie wiping her lips. Laughing, the children ran to hug her. Everyone seemed to be okay. The old woman burped. Suzie and the children turned to face her.

"However did our pizza turn into that horrible thing?" asked Suzie. The woman sighed, and placing her pin back in her hat, she shook her head sadly.

''I told you not to use that herb. Devil's leaf it was, and as you can see, it only brings trouble.'' She walked to the door and left but not before turning at the last minute to flash them a smile.

''It was a hideous monster, there was no mistaking that.'' She paused and looked to the floor.'' But hell, was it a tasty one!''

The Blueberry Thief

A single house martin sat on his window sill, tapping its beak against the glass in a way that said, 'I see you in there, come on out into the garden.' Mr McGovern regarded the bird with indifference then turned his back on it. He didn't wish to go into the garden; he hated the garden. He took very little interest in it now. Once upon a happy time, the garden had been one of his two greatest loves—his other love had been his wife, Rosalie. Now they were both lost to him.

Mr McGovern couldn't bear to see the garden overgrown and dishevelled-looking so he paid one of the local boys to mow it whenever it needed it. It needed it now. During the warm summer days the grass and everything else had grown rapidly. He twisted a ring on his little finger. It was his wife's. He ran the tip of his fingernail in the many scratches that were etched on the outside of it. The ring became scuffed while diving in the Red Sea. That had been a wonderful holiday. He smiled sadly; he missed her so much.

The house martin reappeared. This time it sat on his garden bench. It chirruped merrily. Mr McGovern scowled. The bench was where he and his wife sat most often—laughing and teasing and sharing their news and their dreams. The sun came out from behind a cloud and the bird took off, his rump, a whizzing flash of white. Mr McGovern raised an eyebrow. He pushed his face next to the window for a better look. The cheeky creature had made for his blueberry bush. The man narrowed his eyes. He tapped at the window to try and scare the bird away. Why was he bothered by this? After all, he didn't need the garden anymore; hardly gave it a glance——someone should enjoy it. But somehow, on this particular day he couldn't stop thinking thought about it. The garden and everything about it just played in his mind.

Suddenly, he felt compelled to venture outside. Was it the churlish nature of the bird who had tapped at his window then stolen his blueberries or was it something else? He wasn't sure. He wasn't sure of anything anymore. Except that at that very moment he wanted to enter the garden. He burst out the back door and before he could back away and reconsider his decision, he found himself standing among the ankle-high grass staring at his new-found, feathered acquaintance.

''Off with you.'' He shooed the bird away from the bush. It made for the sky, sailing over the wall into another garden. Mr McGovern looked around him. Despite the long grass and the untrimmed shrubs, the garden was still rather pretty; purple clover, poppies and daisies littered the grass, rose bushes tangled about the apple trees and strawberry plants dripped with fat, ripened fruits. He closed his eyes, feeling the sun on his skin and listened. The breeze fluttered the leaves. Bees buzzed. And the house martin tweeted somewhere. His fingers found his wife's wedding ring and he twisted it again.

With energy he'd forgotten he had, he pulled his jumper off and took out his lawnmower, rake, shears and shovel and set about tidying the garden. After some time, he found a welt forming on his finger. The wedding ring rubbed next to it painfully. He slipped it off and placed it on the outside window sill.

The house martin returned suddenly and landed on the handle of his shovel. The man was cutting away the rose bushes. He eyed the bird then slowly turned himself around to face the creature fully. The bird whistled again, 'I knew you'd come out sir. This is such beautiful garden. You'd be foolish to miss out on it.' The man smiled and looked back down at his roses. When he gazed up again, the bird was gone.

Later that evening Mr McGovern jumped suddenly off the couch as he thought about his stupidity. It was well into the evening for the sky had since glowed in a purple-orange haze giving way to the dark night, when he remembered the wedding ring. He had left it sitting on the outside window sill. Grabbing a torch, he raced to the garden. It wasn't there. He paced through the grass looking for the ring, hoping it had fallen nearby. He couldn't bear to lose it——it was all he had left of his late wife. After an hour, he still hadn't found it. He went to bed that night with a heavy heart.

The summer was long and hot. Mr McGovern spent all his time enjoying the garden; keeping the grass short and neat, watering, weeding and tending the plants and flowers until the whole garden had been transformed back into the beautiful space he once used to share with his Rosalie. Contented, he sat on their bench and stared at the sky. In his head, he heard his wife's voice, ''you can find happiness everywhere——you just have to look.''

Often he would see the house martin but he never again scared the bird away. Associating the bird with the day he lost the ring, he squeezed his finger, the place where it once was.

Summer gave way to autumn and little by little Mr McGovern saw less and less of the friendly bird. One day in late September, while digging up potatoes, he was startled when a bird's nest fell from the eaves of his house. Delicately, he picked it up. It was a well-formed ball, small and round. Straw and bits of dried twigs stuck out from a single hole in the centre. He gently pulled them out. Hidden inside them was something shiny. The old man gasped—his wife's wedding ring, the distinctive scratches on the exterior clearly visible. Mr McGovern held it up to the sun. It glinted brightly. His face creased to a smile as he placed the ring on his finger then picked up his shovel and got on with his digging.

Printed in Great Britain
by Amazon